BreezyGirl

BreezyGirl

Esthela Núñez Franco

BreezyGirl
Copyright © 2019 by Esthela Núñez Franco. All rights reserved.

No part of this publication may be reproduced, stored in a retrieval system or transmitted in any way by any means, electronic, mechanical, photocopy, recording or otherwise without the prior permission of the author except as provided by USA copyright law.

This novel is a work of fiction. Names, descriptions, entities, and incidents included in the story are products of the author's imagination. Any resemblance to actual persons, events, and entities is entirely coincidental.

The opinions expressed by the author are not necessarily those of URLink Print and Media.

1603 Capitol Ave., Suite 310 Cheyenne, Wyoming USA 82001
1-888-980-6523 | admin@urlinkpublishing.com

URLink Print and Media is committed to excellence in the publishing industry.

Book design copyright © 2019 by URLink Print and Media. All rights reserved.

Published in the United States of America

ISBN 978-1-64367-770-5 (Paperback)
ISBN 978-1-64367-771-2 (Hardback)
ISBN 978-1-64367-769-9 (Digital)

15.08.19

For my father, Isidro Núñez Ramirez, and husband, Dale E. Schnee.

"Cassie, are you ready?" asked Victoria.

Yes! Cassie told her by responding with a loud and clear neigh.

The pony shook off her body as she raced toward the gate to meet Victoria. Cassie was Victoria's favorite pony! Victoria had many horses, but she frequently chose to ride Cassie. It was easy to do. Cassie was a very talented jumper pony. She was fast, and she could jump very high. Cassie was never afraid of any obstacles.

She and Victoria had been together for many years. Cassie thought of Victoria as more than just her rider; she was her sister. Although horses could not talk, the pony's love for her rider was obvious. Cassie always took care of her rider. Cassie loved and protected her, just as a sister would.

Victoria opened the stall door and put the halter on Cassie to lead her out. Cassie was surprised when Victoria handed her lead rope to her father so he could load her into a horse trailer. *I do not recognize this trailer!* Cassie thought as she began to pull away.

This was the horse trailer of a stranger. It had a strange smell and was full of horses she did not know. Cassie felt very nervous and concerned. A few minutes later, the pony realized what was happening as the trailer started to move.

Slowly, Cassie was separated from her sister.

Victoria waved at Cassie and said, "You be a good girl!"

Cassie did not understand why a stranger took her or why Victoria let her go. All she knew was that her pony heart was broken.

Meanwhile, far away from Victoria's house, a storm was building up on the front porch of a modest country home. The storm was the sound of laughter coming from a happy girl.

"Lola! Lola! Look what I got today!" said Stella.

Lola was an African gray parrot who had no trouble repeating and mimicking Stella's voice. The storm would get louder and louder.

"My friend Heather gave me her show coat, pants, boots, and this fancy show helmet. She gave me everything, Lola! Everything! She said she didn't need these riding clothes anymore, and I can keep them so I can ride horses. Do you like them, girl?"

Stella thought now she could ride horses just like Heather and win lots of ribbons. She kept imagining how fun it would be to compete in a horse show. She thought her dream of riding horses was finally becoming a reality.

"Horses, horses, horses," Lola kept repeating. She had found a new tune and new words to sing. "Horses, horses, horses."

Lola's song made Stella's smile even bigger and brighter. Stella sang with Lola, "Horses, horses, horses. Horses, horses, horses. Horses, horses, horses. Horses, horses, horses!"

Stella had a plan on how she was going to get a horse. The plan was to walk down to the neighbor's farm and simply buy one of his horses. *Easy enough,* she thought. She saved her allowance for a month, and now, with a complete horse-show outfit, all she needed was the horse.

As she started walking down the road to Mr. Dale's farm, her dog Junior joined her. Junior accompanied Stella everywhere. Things were always better when Junior was around.

"Good boy, Junior. Maybe you can help me pick out a horse," she told him as the two of them kept walking. Stella was determined to buy and ride a horse. Besides her family, she loved horses and dogs the most.

Mr. Dale lived on a farm down the road from Stella's house. He was a horse trader who had many horses—all sizes and all colors. With so many horses to choose from, Stella thought this would be a simple decision.

Once she got to the farm, Junior quickly forgot about helping her pick out a horse. He left Stella behind as he ran ahead to play with the other dogs. Mr. Dale had many horses, and he had just as many dogs! He had a big dog named Sage, an even bigger dog called Tippy, a short-legged corgi named Rudy, and a very sleepy beagle Mr. Dale referred to as Mr. Jackson.

"Mr. Dale! Mr. Dale!" Stella yelled from across the field. "I am here to buy a horse."

Mr. Dale quickly stopped his tractor and walked toward Stella. "You want to buy a horse, kiddo? Do you know how to ride?" he asked with a surprised look on his face.

A more surprised Stella responded, "No, but I always wanted to." Catching her breath, she continued. "My friend gave me one of her old riding outfits and a helmet, and I am ready to ride. I brought my money too."

Mr. Dale responded, "I see. Where is your dad?" Stella needed to have an adult present to buy a horse.

As she waited patiently for her father to get home from work, she kept thinking about what to tell him. She would start by saying that she needed a horse to go with her horse-show outfit. That was easy enough, she thought.

After talking to her father, Stella heard answers that were hard for her to understand.

"Daughter, we don't have money to buy a horse," said her dad.

Stella felt her heart getting heavy as tears filled her eyes.

After watching her reaction, her father quickly added, "I tell you what. Tomorrow, we can both talk to Mr. Dale. Maybe he can let you ride one of his horses until we have enough money saved to buy one."

Stella had a big smile again. She knew she had the best father. He always found a way to make her happy.

After Stella's father spoke with Mr. Dale, he agreed to let Stella ride his older brown mare named Lily Lope. "Now, just be careful with Lily. Have your dad help you, okay?" Mr. Dale advised as he was helping Stella and her dad walk Lily to their farm. "She is a good mare, but she will test you. Just let her know you are the leader, and you will be okay."

Stella was very nervous about having to be the leader. Before that day, nobody had asked her to be a leader. She was not sure how to do it or where to start. To her, it seemed like a very difficult thing to do.

Lily was finally home, and Stella was ready to start riding. All she wanted to do was ride a horse in her new horse-show outfit. She planned to go to shows and win ribbons.

Stella and the mare did well for a while. Until one day, something unexpected happened.

Lily accidentally tripped, making Stella lose her seat and fall. She landed by Lily's front legs. The mare immediately protected Stella by quickly hopping over her so she would not be stepped on.

This accident terrified Stella. She froze in fear. Her father saw the accident and quickly ran to help her. Luckily, both Lily and Stella were okay.

Stella was so scared that she could not get close to Lily anymore. She was too scared to touch the mare and even more terrified to ride her. She told her father she was done with horses.

As always, her dog Junior would be by her side to comfort her. Over the next few weeks, Stella felt sad and very scared. "How could this have happened?" she asked her father one day.

He always explained things in a way Stella could understand.

"Accidents happen when riding horses, Stella. Lily didn't trip intentionally. Horses are live animals." She listened quietly, trying to understand what her father said. "It's not Lily's fault. Don't be mad at her. And more important, don't be scared of her. Sometimes horses teach us to be strong."

After the riding accident with Lily, Stella felt devastated. Many times, she told her dad that she would never ride again. Stella did not think she could be a leader or be strong—until one day.

"Mr. Dale! Mr. Dale! I am ready for another horse!" Stella yelled once again from across the field.

Once again, Mr. Dale stopped doing chores and asked the question she hated the most. "Hi, Stella. Where is your dad?"

Stella realized this horse business seemed to work only between grownups. She must have her father talk with Mr. Dale.

After Mr. Dale and her father spoke, they agreed to have Stella try out another horse. This time, it would be a smaller mare named Gray.

Gray was an honest and hardworking mare. She loved her job best when she ran barrels and on open pastures. Mostly, she loved to participate in gymkhana events. She only had one speed, and that was a *gallop!* Gray always behaved as if she thought, *Why walk when you can run?* That was simply Gray's personality.

Before she came to Mr. Dale's farm, kids rode Gray. She loved to go fast for her smaller riders. Stella quickly got excited about the idea of riding a smaller mare—especially a mare that was used to being around kids. "This will be easy! Easy!" she told the mare as she petted her.

A few days later, Gray moved to Stella's farm. With her father always by her side, he started teaching her once again how to handle a horse. He taught her the same way his father had taught him in old Mexico. Her father always told stories about him and his father and the horses they rode at their family ranch. Stella loved to hear the stories. They gave her the opportunity to learn more about the grandfather she never knew. Unfortunately, he passed shortly after she was born.

Her father treated horses just as he treated her: with patience and love. Things between Gray and Stella were going great, until one day, Stella felt confident enough to take Gray out to a public arena. With no trailer or pickup, that was no easy task. Stella and her father had to walk a couple of miles to the county fairgrounds.

Once they got there, Stella started riding Gray. As soon as the mare entered the arena, Stella felt Gray pacing faster and faster. Gray must have thought she was asked to run barrels! Before Stella could react, Gray suddenly started galloping toward a barrel.

Not knowing how to stop her, Stella got very scared and lost control of the mare. As she kept leaning forward and pulling on the reins at the same time, Gray became more confused.

Her father, watching from a distance, yelled, "Sit back! Sit back! Sit back on the saddle, Stella!"

She quickly sat back, making Gray come to a complete stop. It was similar to a stop made by a car with good brakes!

However, Stella did not have good brakes on her seat. She quickly fell forward and landed on the ground just a few feet in front of Gray.

The mare stood there waiting patiently for her rider to get up. "Whew!" Stella told her dad. "Good thing I was wearing a helmet!" Although she pretended to be amused, inside she was shaking with fear.

That evening, she told her father she no longer wanted to ride horses. The next day, Stella returned Gray to Mr. Dale's farm. The mare happily ran into the pasture. As he closed the gate, Mr. Dale noticed the look of sadness on Stella's face.

He told her, "Horses are not returnable like clothes that don't fit well." He hoped to catch her attention. She started listening carefully to what Mr. Dale had to say. "I know how much you want to ride. I had many spills when I was a kid. Just do not give up, kiddo. No matter how long it takes, you will would need to be strong and be a leader with any horse."

As Stella walked back home, she thought of those two words that horse people must like to use: strong and leader.

Mr. Dale knew she would be back for another horse. Sure enough, Mr. Dale was right. While doing chores, he heard, "Mr. Dale, Mr. Dale, do you have another horse I can ride?" He looked up, and there she was! Stella was ready to make another horse deal.

As Stella was talking with Mr. Dale, she noticed a weird-looking horse next to her. It had walked slowly all the way from the pasture into the corrals as if it also wanted to be included in the conversation.

Mr. Dale noticed the donkey walking inside the corral. He petted her and asked Stella, "So what was wrong with the horses you've ridden?"

Stella answered honestly, "Well, Lily was too moody, and Gray was just too fast. I just want something I can ride and—"

Mr. Dale quickly interrupted. "You can still ride those mares, Stella. Maybe you just have to give them a chance."

Stella firmly asked, "But why did they try to hurt me?"

Mr. Dale responded, "I know Lily and Gray well enough to say that they would never try to hurt you on purpose. Try to get to know them better. It's just like with new friends in school."

He paused and then continued. "Then also be strong, and be a leader."

Not those words again! Stella thought.

Chores were waiting, and Mr. Dale was about to get back to work when Stella said, "Wait! Who is this? Can I ride it? This is a weird-looking horse."

Mr. Dale responded, "Gracie? She is a donkey. Uh, I guess so. She is broke to ride. You can ride her if you want."

He quickly disclosed, "She is not fast, but she is very easy to ride."

Stella smiled and said, "Great idea! A short and slow donkey."

Mr. Dale and her father spoke later that day.

The following week, Gracie moved to Stella's farm.

More than ever, she felt the support from her father. He continued to help her in this never-ending horse-riding adventure. Only this time, it involved a donkey. A donkey-riding adventure. Stella liked the sound of that. Slow, short, and easy.

"Now Stella, you know Gracie is a donkey and riding her is a lot different than riding a horse," said her father with a long pause. "Donkeys are very smart, and like I always say, if you treat any animal well, they will do the same for you in return."

Unfortunately, the pep talk took longer than the time it took Gracie to dump Stella every time she tried to ride her. Gracie enjoyed dumping Stella in anything that had water, including ditches, puddles, and water troughs.

Actually, Gracie enjoyed dumping Stella anywhere!

Gracie was just not into this riding business. She was happy babysitting Mr. Dale's baby horses out in the pasture. She enjoyed being around mares and their colts or fillies.

Within a week, Gracie happily returned to her old job.

Once more, Stella did not have a horse or donkey to ride. Yet she was very happy not be sitting in a puddle of water.

A few weeks later, Mr. Dale was busy doing farm chores when he thought he heard someone yell, "Mr. Dale! Mr. Dale! Are you around? Are you here? Hello! Hello! Anybody here? Hello? Hello?"

All he could see from far away was a short person with long, brown, curly hair. He got off the tractor, and as he came around a corner, Stella jumped in front to greet him.

Yes, she was back for another horse deal. *Fantastic,* Mr. Dale thought.

Before Mr. Dale could talk, Stella started asking questions. She pointed at a horse. "I'm here because I saw you bring that small horse to your farm yesterday," Stella said as she tried to catch her breath. "Then I just saw some kids riding her today. He is cute! Is he a baby horse? What is his name? Where did he come from? Can I ride him? Is it a girl or boy?"

With many questions, Mr. Dale politely tried to answer each one. After all, chores could wait.

"She is a pony, a pony mare" he said. "She seems very shy. I'm not sure if she will be sold today. Those kids didn't seem to connect with her."

Stella did not know what that meant, but her curiosity was getting to her. She needed to find out more about this horse. She walked over to the corral to get a closer look. To her, it was interesting to know how a pony had made it all the way to Mr. Dale's farm. Mr. Dale had never had any ponies on his farm.

He caught up with Stella at the corral and asked, "Do you want to ride her? She is saddled up!"

Stella told Mr. Dale she was too scared to ride her. She never rode without her father present.

Besides, this pony had an English saddle and Stella was not familiar with English riding. She felt scared of it.

Mr. Dale continued to tell Stella what he knew about the pony. "I was told she came from the east coast to Colorado, but I don't know much about her really. But look! She came with a name on her halter." He handed Stella the fancy leather halter.

She read the name on the plate. "The Breeze?" Stella quickly asked for a clarification "The Breeze? Sounds like the Rain or the Sun. Now I am confused."

Mr. Dale tried to explain. "Nothing to be confused over. She is a show pony, and that is her show name. I was told her first owner called her Cassie for a barn name."

Stella responded, "I don't know what it all means: a show name and barn name? So confusing!"

Stella continued talking. "I just think she is cute—really cute!" She caught her breath and quickly added, "This pony is the cutest horse in your farm. She's so pretty and soft."

Mr. Dale had a feeling where all this talk was going. Another deal between him and Stella's father. Worse yet, possibly another return.

That day, Stella stayed with "the Breeze" for a while. She reached for the pony through the fence to touch her. Stella was very surprised to feel the pony's warm breath on her hand. The pony enjoyed the touch of a young girl's hand.

Stella asked for permission to go inside the corral. Mr. Dale stopped doing chores and watched how the girl and pony interacted with each other. As the pony looked into Stella's eyes, a soft breeze with a flower smell made its way through the farm. It was magical.

"Is your name the Breeze?" whispered Stella.

The pony and Stella stared at each other for a few minutes. She paused for a minute, as if waiting for the pony to answer verbally. She asked again, "Is your name the Breeze or Cassie? Which do you like?"

Stella startled the pony by shouting, "BreezyGirl! That is what I think you should be called!"

She repeated the name with a smile on her face. "BreezyGirl! You look like a BreezyGirl!"

Stella and the pony spent a few more hours together when she heard Mr. Dale ask, "Where is your dad?"

Okay, time to go home, she thought. Mr. Dale had work to do.

She got out of the corral and said, "Thank you, Mr. Dale. I will see you later!"

"Later" in girl time meant minutes later.

"Mr. Dale! My dad and I are here to buy BreezyGirl," said a confident Stella. "BreezyGirl, your pony girl horse. You know, the one you told me I could ride earlier today? Is she sold? She is still here, right?"

As Mr. Dale responded, "No, she is not sold yet," the pony raised her head and listened.

The pony remembered Stella. She let her know by walking toward her to sniff Stella's hand.

"See? She likes me, and she is a girl like me, and we are going to get along just fine. I gave her some treats and I think she remembers. She wants a few more, huh, girl? She loves treats like me."

"I see," said a confused Mr. Dale. He knew Stella was not leaving without the pony. "Well, let me talk with your dad, okay?" He thought he would change her mind by asking, "Don't you think you're a little too big for her?"

Stella quickly responded, "No, she is small but very strong." She acted like a horse breed expert.

Mr. Dale quickly agreed and said, "Yes, you are right, Stella. Ponies can be very strong, and your BreezyGirl seems that way."

That afternoon, Stella made another horse deal. The pony mare would be coming home with her. She thanked her father and Mr. Dale.

As Stella was leaving with the pony, Mr. Dale stopped her and said, "Now remember you have to give her a chance. Talk to her. Let her know what is going on. You have to connect with horses, okay?"

Stella listened carefully as he continued.

"The first thing to do is to get to know each other. This will take time. Also remember to be strong and be a leader."

She thought about it for a second and told him, "Okay, I will try. I promise, Mr. Dale."

Stella quickly led the pony away, not giving Mr. Dale a chance to change his mind about selling BreezyGirl.

"BreezyGirl! Are you ready for a ride?" said Stella as she saddled the pony. "Let's go, girl! Let's see what you can do."

Stella led her into the arena where they could jump cross rails. Without her father present, Stella felt scared to take the pony for ride. However, she did it; she could not wait for her father to get home from work.

"Okay, girl, let's see you jump."

As Stella led the pony into the public arena, BreezyGirl saw the jump cross rails and rushed toward them. She jumped so high and quick that it caused Stella to lose her balance and fall off.

"BreezyGirl! What happened?" asked Stella with a puzzled and scared look on her face. As she got up and dusted herself, she said, "Okay, girl, maybe jumps scare you? Let's just try riding around the arena."

A few minutes later, Stella found herself lying on the ground again and staring at the blue sky. As they started walking along the rail, the pony spun so quickly, making Stella fly off the saddle. BreezyGirl acted as if she was upset about something.

Stella got scared. "Did you get spooked, girl? It's okay," said Stella as she dusted herself again. "Let's try something else."

Stella led her inside a round pen located next to the arena. As she started riding at the walk, BreezyGirl suddenly bolted and bucked. Stella lost her balance and fell yet again.

Three falls in one day. She felt discouraged and did not want to get back on the pony. Stella felt she had no choice but to walk the pony back to the barn.

She decided not to tell her father about what happened that day.

Stella became very quiet and sad. Her fear of horses came back.

She was sad to realize that now she was afraid of this pony. Just like she was with the other horses. Fear was the last thing she wanted to feel.

At first, she thought it would be easier to ride this pony because it was smaller and looked calmer. She wanted to be strong and a leader but felt that she failed with every horse she rode. She did not feel strong and did not feel like a leader.

Stella had hoped BreezyGirl was the last horse she would have to try. All she wanted was to connect and bond with her. She just did not know how to do it.

It had to be the pony's fault. There had to be something wrong with her. She was disappointed in BreezyGirl. This pony was her hope and dream. Stella was just a girl with a dream of being in horse shows.

She felt this pony was too scary to ride. Stella did not want to tell her dad how she felt, and she certainly did not want to return another horse to Mr. Dale.

Over the next few days, Stella became sadder and felt lonely.

This was also how the pony felt.

A few months passed, and Stella continued to be scared of the pony. She was too scared to get close to her.

One day during breakfast, her father asked, "What are we going to do with that pony? If you are not going to ride it, we need to do something with her."

Stella quietly listened and said, "I know, Papa. I am just scared." Her eyes quickly began to fill up with tears. "I know we don't have the money to keep her. I am so sorry about all of this. She just really scares me."

Her dad always had a solution. He thought for a minute and told her, "Maybe we can find someone to help you learn to ride."

He took a short pause and said, "I never took lessons, but maybe they can help you. I could do for some farm work in exchange for your riding lessons. I am sure Mr. Dale knows someone we can ask to teach you to ride."

Her father patiently waited for her response and hoped he could stop Stella's heart from hurting. He did not want to see his daughter sad and definitely did not want to see her scared of the animals she loved the most.

Horses.

She wiped her tears and gave her dad a big hug.

"It will be okay," he said. "Someday you will not be afraid. You'll see. Someday you will be strong."

Her father was right; that day came soon enough. Stella felt something she had never felt before. She felt the need to talk to the pony heart-to-heart.

"BreezyGirl" said Stella quietly as she walked toward the barn. "BreezyGirl are you there? Can I talk to you?"

The pony slowly made her way toward Stella as if she also wanted to talk. Stella felt that she needed to let the pony know what was going on with her and how her fear of riding kept her away. She put the halter on BreezyGirl and took her for a walk.

As both girls walked, Stella asked the pony to help her. She asked her to be patient while she learned to become a better rider. Stella asked BreezyGirl to help her not be afraid.

"BreezyGirl, I want to tell you that my dad is helping me find riding lessons. If I ride better and won't get so scared, would that be better for you? We can find someone to help us."

The pony briefly stopped sniffing Stella's hand and raised her head to pay attention, as if she wanted to hear more about the plan.

Stella added, "Maybe if I don't get scared, you don't get scared.

We can be partners like in school, or friends, or maybe even like sisters? I can learn to be strong and be a leader for you. We are about the same age. We can be sisters and partners."

As they continued to walk, the pony suddenly stopped. *Sisters?* BreezyGirl remembered what this word meant.

Yes! Sisters! The pony knew exactly what this word sounded like and what it meant. BreezyGirl could not believe it! Did she just hear Stella say the word *sisters*? She did not want to be mistaken. The pony remembered what it was like to have a "sister." She once had a "sister" when she lived with Victoria.

The pony put her head on Stella's shoulder. This was her way of telling Stella she understood and also wanted to be close like sisters.

Stella, surprised at the pony's reaction, asked her, "What, girl? Are you itchy? Do you want me to scratch you? How about a hug—a sister hug?"

The pony heard the word *sister* once again. This time, she was not shy about expressing her happiness.

She expressed how happy she was by running, bucking, rolling on the ground, and occasionally passing gas! Stella could not stop laughing from watching BreezyGirl's reaction. She had never seen a horse act like that. These were all signs of a horse that felt good.

The pony had not felt this happy in so long. This was a miracle.

She now knew that she could have another sister in Stella. She did not think it could happen again, but it did—just like magic.

They were both part of each other's lives now. The pony even liked her new name: BreezyGirl.

Life was good again, just as it should be.

Over the next few months, Stella took riding lessons from a horse trainer who lived nearby. Riding lessons helped her in many ways. She grew more confident and became less scared. She became a much better rider. Stella learned to be strong and be a leader for BreezyGirl.

This allowed her to participate in local shows and riding events. Sometimes, the hardest thing about these events was keeping Stella's hair neatly tucked under a helmet! These girls even had that in common—they both had a lot of hair! Stella did not care what her hair looked like. She was happy. That was all that mattered to her. Her dream had come true.

Stella's father and Mr. Dale were happy to know that these two girls had found each other. It took time and patience to form a bond. An unbreakable bond between horse and rider.

Stella and BreezyGirl had become sisters.

Everyone enjoyed watching BreezyGirl and Stella ride and jump logs out in the pasture. It looked like these girls always had fun.

Sometimes, all the dogs would come along for one long trail ride. It would get quite crowded! All the dogs would get tired quickly, except for that short-legged corgi. He had strong legs and could go on for miles!

Stella's life changed when she listened to her father and to Mr. Dale. Both men shared with her how they found love and formed a bond with their horses. They gave her advice by sharing their personal stories.

They taught her to connect with BreezyGirl in a magical way. The unique magic that could only happen between a horse and rider. They also showed her that with love and patience, anything was possible. They coached her on how to be a strong leader.

She realized how lucky she was to have the gift of love. The gift of love that could happen between a horse and rider.

Over the next several years, their bond became stronger. They became inseparable. BreezyGirl and Stella knew each other's needs.

They continued to travel to horse shows and participated in many different riding events. Sometimes, they won ribbons at shows. Other times, they did not. There were good rides and bad rides.

Often, they just rode with friends who lived near their farm or simply went for long walks at the lake.

BreezyGirl loved nature. As all unicorns did.

They had each other. They never felt sad and lonely again.

As always, Stella's father continued to be by her side, guiding her in a way only a father could: with patience and love.

Stella made a promise to BreezyGirl that she would keep for life.

She promised BreezyGirl that she would never leave her and that they would always be together.

"We are sisters," she said, "and family is forever."

Stella once told BreezyGirl, "I want you to live forever."

In her own way, BreezyGirl responded, "As long as I am in your heart, I will."

www.ingramcontent.com/pod-product-compliance
Ingram Content Group UK Ltd.
Pitfield, Milton Keynes, MK11 3LW, UK
UKHW060137240426
12048UKWH00002B/82